NIEK

LEAVE THE BIRD SAMPLE

NAMAN DHIMAN

Contents

Foreword *v*

1. Chapter O : Before You Read 1
2. Chapter 1: May 3
3. Chapter 2 : Visa 4
4. Chapter 3 : Chale Delhi 5
5. Chapter 4 : Kahaniya 7
6. Intro/sample Ends 8

DISCLAIMER

Part 2

Part 3

Part 4

Part 5

Part 6

Part 7

Part 8

Part 9

Part 10

Part 11

Part 12

Part 13

Part 14

Part 15

Part 16

Part 17

Contents

Part 18

Part 19

Foreword

When you are in a hole...

Most projects start well, and with perfectly good interaction.

This is a small intro book of our next story from KHOYA series

CHAPTER ONE

CHAPTER O : BEFORE YOU READ

The story begins from a 12year old young boy. Before stepping into teenage he follows offline meets,games but after his entry on social media. Some sort of things happen that he would have never thought.

"Most of things you worry about never happens" as well as "A lot can happen in one year".

These two lines will carry forward the book till the end.

The name of the boy is Rohan who was then studying in 7th standard academic year 2019-20 Month of May he found some random guys on Instagram.

Respectively: Jatin Shukla, Aryan Pal, he follows his online life more than spending time at home with elders.Then he started to play online shooting games with his instagram friends.

And those friends continuosly asked him to come over thier city.

AND...

NIEK

2

CHAPTER TWO

CHAPTER 1: MAY

2May ye date shyad mene apne calendar m mark krli h cause is din muje kuch dost mile or aise wese dost nhi galiz dost.... sounds funny but that's the truth and I am Rohan. Wo kehte h na `Aage chalkar yehi time yaad ayega '.....

May ke end tak aate aate humne ek dusre ke baare m boht kuch jaan lia Jese ki wo merse 10 saal bde h. Khyal m yehi sb aya ki dost to dost hove h kisi sidefilm ke kisi dialogue ki trah.

Par han is mahine ne meko boht kuch dia apne saath aage lejane ke lie.

Ab chahe usko as a present leke chale ya future ye tense aakhir hai konsa ye to

meko bhi nhi pta tha.

CHAPTER THREE

CHAPTER 2 : VISA

Chapter 2 may afsos is baat k h ye kahani thoda aage agyi h.Kyuki kuch chize

aisi h jo btai bhi nhi ja skti. Aage bdhte bdhte september ho chla tha.wahi

kachhe sapne wahi kachhi mat ke saath m aage badh rha tha . Ofcourse papers k

mahol hota h some serious tensions as we can say but after the mid term exam .

Meko bulaya gya frr se delhi mere online friends ke traf se ,Lagatar invitation chla

aarha tha pichle 4 5 mahine se or ab mna bhi nhi hua .

Kyuki itna frankly speaking baatein hoti thi group m . Par strangers par bhrosa nhi krna

chahiye ofcourse .Frr bhi try kia ghr se kisi trahh rone ki acting krke permssion mili .Surprisingly m khud nhi janta permission mili kese vo bhi indian parents se.Becoz Permission lena utna hi mushkil h jitna binod ko dekh rha h na binod bolna.

Aur agar kisi or ki kismt itni achhi ho to usko pkka visa lagne jesa fel ayega kyuki canada to chordo unhe to pichli gali ke pintu kabadi pe nhi jaane ko milta..

CHAPTER FOUR

CHAPTER 3 : CHALE DELHI

Aakhir vo log muje lene aane waale they ek gut feeling thi ki sahi ho rha h na jo ho rha h.Par khushi bhi thi ki vo aa rhe h or aise kisi ko bhi judge krne ki to adat hoti h specially Indians m.Or aakhirkar vo din aa gya jab vo log pehli baar mere ghr aaye.Surprise package tha ye sb mere lie ki muje "MERE DOST" specially lene aaye h.Actually baat 2 log ki hui thi. Aaye they 3.Jatin Shukla,Aryan Pal or Rohit Singh. Pta h ye sb mere lie unique or itna special kyu tha kyuki tab muje vishvash ho gia tha ki ye kahani boht lambi jayegi.Rohit Singh inhe ke group ke member or inke bachpan ke dost Mera to chal hi rha h. M gaadi m jese hi betha muje itna pta lag gya tha ki m safe hu cause jin logon ki mulaqat hi "Naam ke piche ladte hue" hui h unse or kya hi expect kr skte h.Actually jaate hue bhi ek kaand hua unhone gaadi le jaake no parking zone m khadi ki thi.Gaadi tow krne waale aa hi rhe they ki.in logon ne marigold flower ki mala "GENDE KA PHOOL" khrid ke unke worker ko pehna di.Yaha se m ye sb dekh or sun smjh ke ek hi chiz kehna chahunga.

CHALE DELHI?

....

....

CHAPTER FIVE

CHAPTER 4 : KAHANIYA

Ek kahani likhne m kam se kam 6 mahine 1 saal lag jaate h even agar vo kahani man m ho tabh bhi.Par us kahani ko jeene m "SIRF EK SECOND" shyad kuch unme se m bhi jeene wala tha. Kyuki delhi to hum aa hi gye they bss. Raste m humne bss gaane sunte sunte vibe kia koi logical ya senseful baat ni hui 1 2 ko chord ke.

Jab hum pahuche to ....

JATIN SHUKLA: Chlo pahuch gye Rohan.

AT that moment when I came out and went in its just crazy lyk ghr ke andar enter krte hi mene 3 se 4 logon ko sofe pe pade pade movie dekhte hue dekha .

PICHE SE AWAAZ AAYI...

ARYAN PAL: Ruk kyu gye chlo naa ab andar *BAKCHODI* ke lie aaye h shuru ho jayo.....

Us moment pe m sirf mze krna ye sb hi sochra tha but shyad kuch kahani bhi ban rhi thi jo muje aaj tak achhe se yaad h

CHAPTER SIX

INTRO/SAMPLE ENDS

THIS IS THE INTRODUCTION SHORT BOOK FOR THE UPCOMING STORY FROM KHOYA SERIES IT WAS DECIDED TO LAUNCH THE FIRST BOOK ON 17 AUGUST BUT DUE TO SOME CHANGES IN PLANS, TILL FURTHER UPDATE i.e MAIN BOOK WILL BE AVAILABLE THIS YEAR BUT NOT WITH EXACT DATE.

DISCLAIMER

KRIPYA CHUTIYE LOG IS BOOK KO NA PDHE YE KAHANI UNKE LIE NHI H DHANYAWAD.

“KAHANI KO SOCHNE SE JYADA USE LIKHNE M TIME LGTA H”

SOMETIMES THE STORY IS IN FRONT OF YOU BUT YOU CAN’T WRITE THE WHOLE.

WORKING ON THE BOOK FROM FEBRAURY

BUT STILL LEFT WITH SOME CHANGES .

Stay commited to your dreams

They are more loyal than

Human beings.

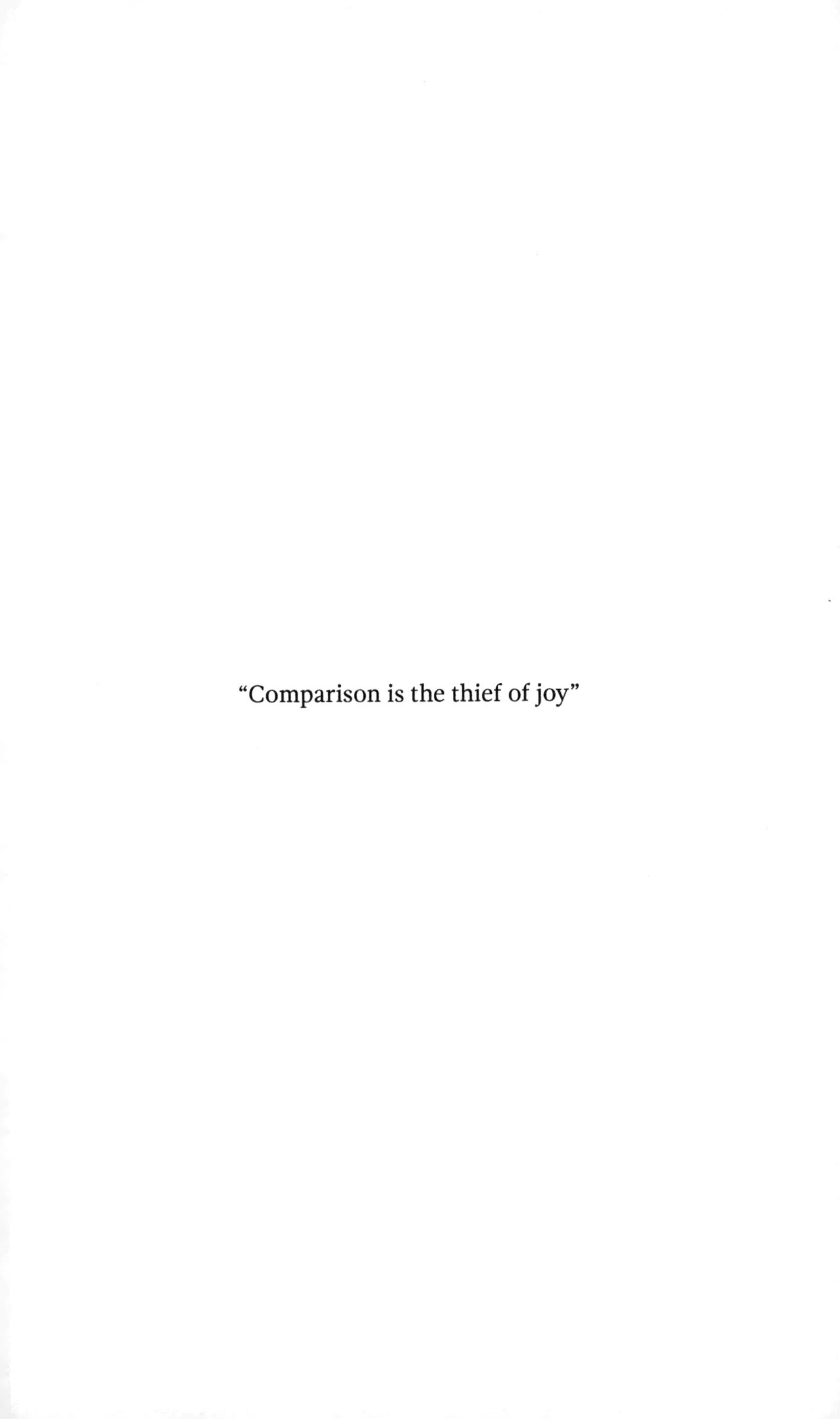

"Comparison is the thief of joy"

“ If I read a book and it makes my whole body so cold no fire can ever warm me,

I know that is poetry. “

FAITH............ ......

NIEK

VICTOR OF PEOPLE

ELEVATE

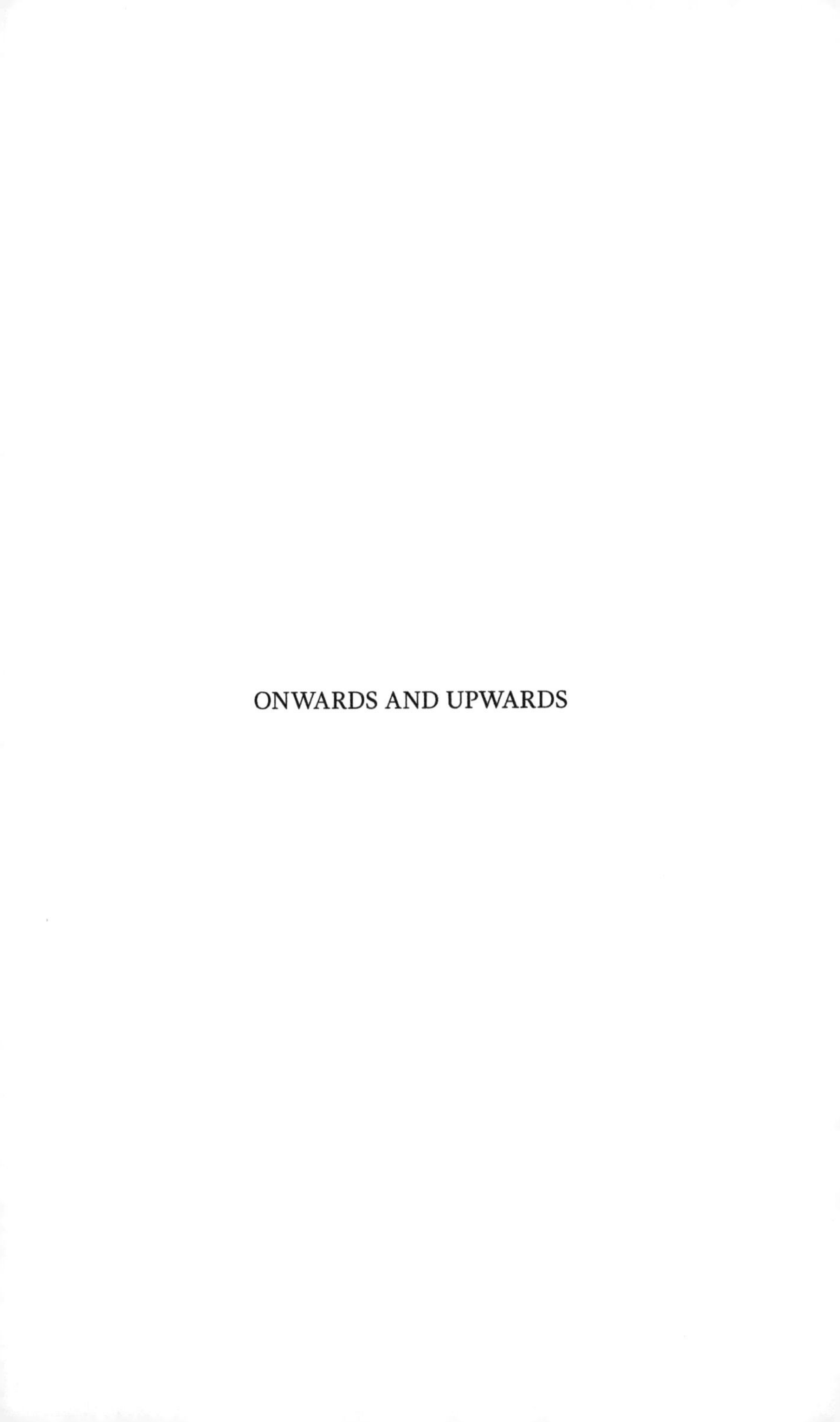

ONWARDS AND UPWARDS

“I AM NOT AFRAID OF STORMS, FOR I AM LEARNING HOW TO SAIL MY SHIP.” ...

YOU WILL FACE MANY DEFEATS IN LIFE, BUT NEVER LET YOURSELF BE DEFEATED. .....

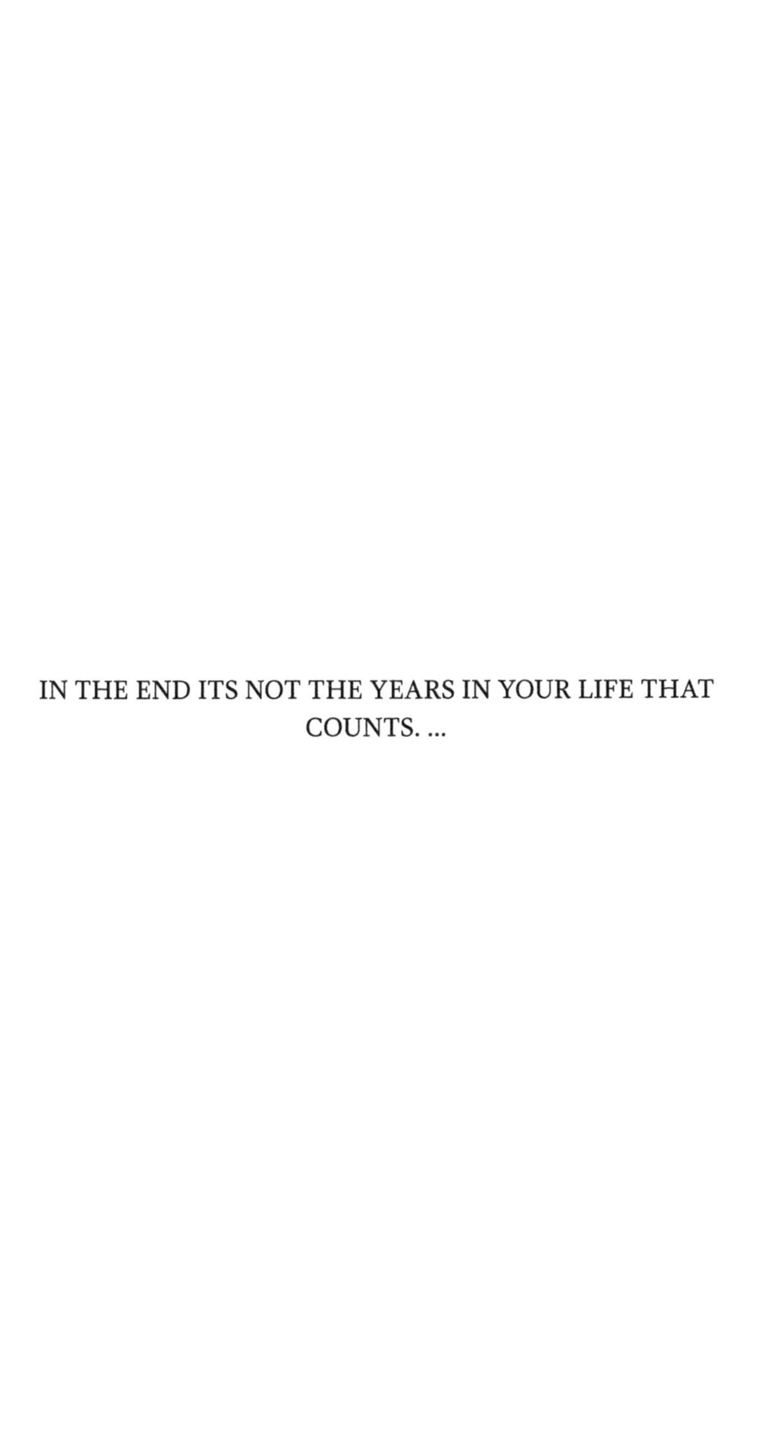

IN THE END ITS NOT THE YEARS IN YOUR LIFE THAT COUNTS. ...

...

SO MANY BOOKS SO LITTLE TIME.

DON'T TELL PEOPLE YOUR PLANS. .....

WHERE NOTHING GOES RIGHT GO LEFT. ...

TRY AND TRY

"YOU MUST BE THE CHANGE YOU WISH TO SEE IN THE WORLD."

TRY TO BE RAINBOW IN SOMEONE'S CLOUD. ....

9 798888 052082

Printed by Libri Plureos GmbH in Hamburg,
Germany